The Real Life of Shadows

Library of Congress Cataloging-in-Publications Data

Frémon, Jean, 1946–
    [Vraie nature des ombres. English]
    The real life of shadows / Jean Fremon ; translated from the French by
Cole Swensen.
        p. cm.
    ISBN 978–0–942996–67–8
    I. Swensen, Cole, 1955– II.Title.
    PQ2666.R37V7313 2009
    848'.91409–dc22

                                                                    2008043572

The Post-Apollo Press
35 Marie Street
Sausalito, California 94965

Book design by Simone Fattal
Cover drawing by Etel Adnan

Typeset by Kathleen Wilkinson
in Perpetua for the text
and Arno Pro and Minion for the titling

Printed in the United States of America on acid-free paper.

Jean Frémon

The Real Life of Shadows

translated from the French by

Cole Swensen

THE POST-APOLLO PRESS

Contents

Giotto's O

Stefano, emissary of the pope, sang as he walked along, and from the hills of Oltrarno, the coo-coo replied. Primula brightened the path through the oaks bustling with starlings, and a litter of young black boar scattered into the undergrowth. The abbot Stefano sang.

On his way back from Siena, he had crossed San Donato, stopping to fill his gourd at the fountain of Tavarnelle, and passed the night in San Casciano at the Order of Friars Minor. In the morning, he'd passed through Galluzo to buy a loaf of bread and some sweet onions. And now he'd arrived—from the top of the hill, he could already see the Arno down in the valley and the towers of Florence beyond.

Under his arm, he carried a large roll of drawings by the best painters in Siena. Ugolino had given him a journey of the magi, Simone, a baptism of Christ, and Ambrosio, an annunciation, to mention only the most illustrious, while their students had outdone themselves to show how well they'd help their masters if the latter were chosen.

For the pope had come up with a project: frescoes for Saint Peter's in Rome, frescoes that would enlighten the conscience through image, that would render faith irrefutable. He'd asked the abbot Stefano to visit all the studios in Tuscany in search of the very best. Mediocrity simply does not convince, said the pope. His secret wish was to bend genius to his will.

Stefano stopped at the top of the hill; the sun had disappeared behind the ridgeline, and night was beginning to fall. He tucked his roll into the fork of an olive tree to protect it from the morning dew, and, spreading his cloak out on the ground, sat down to eat his bread and onions, drink the water from Tavarnelle, say his prayers, and go to sleep.

In his dreams, he saw the most beautiful frescoes imaginable. He no longer distinguished the golden halos from sunsets or the coats of the soldiers sleeping at the foot of the cross from simple rocks. The crucified body hung among the trees, and Gabriel, lily in hand, was more real than any image ever could have made him. He saw the monk Francis preaching to the birds gathered in a circle at his feet; he saw the night of the magi and the luminous star above them.

In the morning, Stefano, having slept in a fresco, woke up into a fresco. Cypresses, silhouetted, stood cut out against the sky, and three larks argued over the crumbs of the Galluzo loaf. His back was stiff. He picked up his coat. Was it he or his painted shadow that then descended the hill with a rickety step toward the bridge that crossed the Arno? Night had not yet entirely left him; exhaustion held him in a lightly luminous fever. He was headed toward the studio of Ambrogiotto di Bondone, student of Cimabue, whose reputation had begun to spread beyond the borders of Tuscany.

It was said that Giotto, always a clown, had once painted a fly on the nose of a portrait that Cimabue was working on. The master, returning to his painting and simply thinking that the fly had been attracted by the egg in the tempera, tried several times to brush it away before he realized the trick.

Lifting the bronze lion head and letting it fall, the abbot knocked at the painter's door. Giotto di Bondone did not take off his hat. He was an ugly man, and generally disagreeable. Stefano explained the great plans of the papacy, emphasizing the honor of the invitation, and then spoke highly of the Sienese painters' enthusiasm. Giotto said nothing.

Leaving the abbot on the threshold, he took a sheet of paper out of a trunk, dipped his brush in red and, with a single movement of his wrist, traced a perfect circle without taking his elbow from his side. He then handed the drawing to the abbot saying, There you are.

Stefano, thinking this a joke, replied, Great halo, but it's missing a saint. Then he added, Do you think that can compete with the work of the heirs to the great Byzantine style? Here in this roll, I have a journey of the magi, all three of them with their horses, their donkeys laden with gifts, the star guiding them. I have a baptism of Christ; he's up to his waist in water, and the painter has rendered it so clear that you can see the holy virility between the Savior's legs, and I have an annunciation that shows the Virgin, terrorized by the appearance of the archangel, clutching at a column for support. Their details grasp it all—doctrine, tradition, and nascent innovation. Who do you think you are to scorn such an opportunity?

I mean no scorn, said Giotto, laying his drawing on top of the kings, the baptism, and the archangel. "Show this to the one who sent you, and tell him what you have seen."

So Stefano, though with great misgivings, did.

Yet when they saw the audacity of that perfect circle and heard how it had been drawn, the pope and his advisors saw instantly that Giotto surpassed all the Sienese. They called him to Rome, covered him with gold, and commissioned him to do five scenes from the life of Christ for the ceiling of Saint Peter's. People came from all over Italy to admire them.

"Rounder than Giotto's O" became the term for a dullard who could be easily duped. In Tuscan, the same word is used to indicate both a circle and a limited mind.

On the Coast

Yves Klein, having painted vertical, horizontal, large, small, medium, square, rectangular, and oblong paintings in the same uniform blue, was unsatisfied. Go beyond art, he told himself, as he walked restlessly up and down the Promenade des Anglais. Go beyond art, he repeated as he stretched out on the sand, one arm under his head, his knee bent. He dreams. He doesn't go to sleep; he watches the sky. How pure it is today, a great, cloudless expanse of blue with no visible limit. It's a monochrome, he thinks, the biggest and the most beautiful blue monochrome ever. It's mine: I thought it, and thus I have done it; all I have to do is sign it. And mentally, he adds his signature and the date to the back of the sky and dozes off, happy and proud.

Three seagulls cross the sky from left to right. A Roman would have seen this as a bad omen. The inauspicious birds screech contentedly. Yves Klein wakes up with a start: How dare you, you filthy fowls, how dare you make holes in my painting, the biggest and most beautiful painting ever.

Not far away, on the other side of the Italian border, Lucio Fontana, who had set his own monochromes vibrating with a single slice or several as precise as a sword's slash—slices like mouths, like vaginas—slipped into a dream that wasn't his own. He said, looking up at the sky: This blue monochrome, which is the biggest and the most beautiful ever, how can I pierce it? How can I make the world's biggest and most beautiful painting mine?

But not everyone can be a bird.

A Meeting at an Intersection

Fear cut through with fervor. Analyzing ambiguities. Running into Emily on the street one spring evening. Other visions of disorder. The infernal divisions of the I. All life is a prison.

Words and the abyss within them. It is raining on a lake. Our story. I could no longer doubt that I was hearing your call.

A triangle is a living mystery. Because its nature is black. Azure, azure, azure.

The Alpine snowbell is a small primulaceae, very slender, very fine, barely as long as your little finger.

"Is there love without a body? Immaterial beauty?"
"You're a monster."

A literary journal doing a special issue on Pierre Jean Jouve had asked me for a contribution, so I'd started rereading his books.

The Beautiful Masks, The Desert World, The Primal Scene. I found myself revolving around an emptiness, ideas dropping away. I started extracting words and phrases and recopying them in order to absorb them absolutely. And then, as if adding yeast, I awkwardly began to lavish them with the care that might allow a text to rise from within.

Sometime later, I found myself in Evreux and, having walked all over the city and visited the museum and the cathedral, I went to a small restaurant for lunch. I'd chosen it for its quiet air, and as I waited for my lunch to arrive, I flipped through the second volume of Jouve's complete works, which includes the texts he renounced.

Which is what made me recall the dream. Suddenly and entirely. With the sense that something long buried had been exhumed intact. That night, back at my hotel, I wrote it out in a single sitting as if under dictation.

Picture a street that ends in the country. A true city street with sidewalks and those granite curbs that every child loves to walk along pretending he's a tightrope walker whose foot could, at any moment, and to his ruin, slip and cross that imaginary line that's supposed to separate good from evil. Crossing it would, on the other hand, have very real effects that had been selected in advance from a catalogue of dire consequences. A street that imperceptibly becomes a road lined with fewer and fewer tall buildings, which give way to small houses with side gardens, while weeds start sprouting up in the cracks of the sidewalk.

At a given moment (which is the accepted expression, while actually it's the opposite: the moment is not given; it flits away, evanescent, a moment that memory can never quite pin down), the sidewalk becomes trodden earth; the road narrows, and the grasses merge into a continuous line down the middle while the horizon opens and the sky spreads, and suddenly you're deep in nature and no longer the pawn manipulated on a grid that is the urban pedestrian.

In the dream, the road rose, leading away from the city center, away from a large square lined with movie theaters and restaurants, bustling with the normal evening activity of such a place, with its warm scents of french fries, cigarettes, and cheap perfume. As it left the square, the road got narrower and darker, the streetlights got farther apart, and the bar signs got less lively. Young women with the air of transvestites leaned laughing in doorways, smoking cigarettes and soliciting passers-by. I walked down the middle of the road to stay out of their reach, but their mimicking and grimacing still made me feel an uneasy something between desire and disgust. The smell of the place filled my nostrils. My heart was in my mouth, as they say, and my mouth was dry, my chest tight. I could feel exhaustion rising up my legs, burning in my shoulders. I'd been walking since early afternoon and hadn't eaten since morning. At lunchtime, I'd gone into a bookstore and spent a long time methodically surveying the bookshelves from top to bottom and left to right.

Are you looking for something specific? the clerk had asked.

A surprise, I'd replied.

There are others over there, he'd said, pointing to a back room where the books were piled in stacks almost six feet high, ready to topple over. You had to weave your way among them. And there, almost immediately, I came upon a title that made my heart skip a beat: *La Rencontre au carrefour,* published by Figuiere and Co., 1911. The faded volume was covered in glassine; only the pages of the first section had been cut, and he had signed the title page in the script I knew so well—small and regular, each letter slightly apart. The price of the book, 60 francs, was written in pencil in the upper righthand corner of the flyleaf. I handed the book to the clerk, trembling lest he should refuse to sell it to me, lest he should say that it was a mistake, that the book should not have been put on the pile, and that by deference to the author, who'd wanted the book pulled from circulation, he couldn't possibly let me buy it. I ran through the whole scene in my mind.

Ah yes, was the only thing he'd said, looking me in the eye as he took the money, it's the last one.

I raced outside, tucking the book into the inside pocket of the huge grey raincoat I always wore. I thought I'd stop somewhere for a sandwich, the hour for a real lunch having long passed, and get to reading it as soon as possible. That's what had brought me to the square. There I knew I could find one of those old brasseries that leave you in peace until closing as long as you order a little something from time to time. I knew I'd also be able to find a knife to finish cutting the pages. But when I got to the spot, which turned out to be farther away than I'd remembered, I'd already started feeling that slight euphoria, that unreal sensation that replaces fatigue when you've been walking fast. Endorphins, endorphins, I kept saying to myself, when, without having made a conscious decision, I found myself sitting on a bench in the square just as the sun broke through.

I was leafing through the book, trying, by a few contortions, to read the insides of the uncut sections, when I heard a voice over my shoulder saying:

He shouldn't have written that.

Pardon me?

He shouldn't have written it.

What makes you say that?

He regretted it. He knew perfectly well, or at least in the end he realized, that he shouldn't have written it, and you yourself, you should not be reading it.

But how can you say that? I've been looking for this for ages; I never believed I'd find it—it's a Godsend.

More like bad luck. And now you're going to do something equally bad. Would you read a letter that wasn't addressed to you?

But it's not a matter of that. I simply bought a book ...

Hardly. You know perfectly well that the author wanted to take it all back and yet you're prepared to ignore that—one might even say it titillates you.

But that's all in the past, that was 1911, it's ancient history. Today, we have the right to know.

You're confusing archeology with tomb robbing.

I barely saw the young woman I was talking to; throughout our conversation thus far, I hadn't really looked at her face; I'd responded mechanically to her reproaches, which, far from taking me by surprise, awakened within me an old guilt. But now I saw her face clearly, and I no longer wanted to talk to her, but simply to look. I stood up and walked around the bench in order to sit down next to her. She had nut-brown eyes and very short black hair. She wore a leather jacket and a white T-shirt tucked into jeans. I was deeply moved by her face; it registered both disturbance and determination, both softness and strength, maturity and fantasy, a sheaf of contradictory qualities that amounted to a shimmering space vibrating with intermittent light—or was it simply the rays of the sun striking her face through the leaves of the lime trees stirred by the wind?

All right then, I won't read it, I said taking her hand. I'll be content simply to file it alongside his other books; I have them all, you know—the ones that are authorized and legitimate, the ones you can read without sinning against the spirit. At least you won't take those away from me. And what would reading be without at least a little fetishism: I won't cut the pages, that much I'll promise you; I won't even try to read a few lines, but at least it will be there, standing, pressed between the others, howling its muteness—can we agree on that? May I buy you a cup of coffee? I pointed to one of the cafes on the square. Perhaps over there?

We sat facing each other. In the mirror along the wall, I watched the back of her neck, the way it nestled into the collar of her T-shirt. She told me that her name was Claire, that she came from Dijon, that she was visiting Paris with her mother, who had an appointment with a lawyer to discuss family business.

Now that you've told me what I can't read, you must tell me what I can; what books do you love? (I was only asking in order to get to know this curious woman and her seductively detached charm a little bit better.)

She spoke warmly of various authors I'd never heard of, utterly the opposite of those I usually read, people who wrote pure, lucid stories, free of irony or derision, about experiences in which the daily is transformed by passion, about skies that begin at the top of a trail and unfurl toward the highest mountains, about discovering a nature that fresh and new, about the luminous presence of inspired spaces that radiate a troubling serenity. I felt like I was discovering a whole side of world literature up to then unknown to me.

She spoke of valleys, of mountains, of blue light going into rose, of lakes set in the landscape like, she said, eyes in a face, living lakes because in reflecting the light that fell upon them, they seemed instantly to give back all that the world had given to them. Sils Maria is the only place name that I remember. As for the names of the writers and the titles of their books, I don't recall a single one. Just Sils Maria. I kept watching for the appearance of her tongue between her glistening teeth as she pronounced the name Sils Maria. I was dazzled, struck by love. I couldn't separate what she was saying, which thrilled me, from the mouth and the eyes that were speaking and holding me spellbound. Enthralled and very happy, I was ready to devote my life to her on the spot.

But I suddenly remembered that I'd promised to get together with some friends that evening, and noticing that dusk was falling fast, I told her I'd love to continue our discussion, and that I just had to make a phone call to alter my plans. So I went downstairs to the telephone.

When I came back up a minute later, she'd gone. I ran outside and made a quick tour of the square several times, and, not finding her, I started up the street that climbed the hill, losing myself in it until it was completely dark, always hoping to spot her silhouette in the distance.

The bars became fewer and fewer; the groups of young men, decked out in their make-up and false gaiety, advancing a knee to make their short skirts ride up a bit more, or jutting out their chests to show off their too-perfect breasts, had given way to scattered aging women whispering invitations that even they didn't think anyone would accept.

The noises died down, and a pale gleam deepened. The paved road had gradually given way to stones. Grass was growing along the embankments and birds were chirping in the hedges before I realized that I'd left the city. It was dawn, and a precise light made each object stand out. Even though I knew perfectly well that I'd never been there before, I recognized every detail, the stands of trees, the sky, the hills. The place emanated the exact atmosphere described by my lost friend as we'd sat face to face. I didn't even know her last name. I planned to return to that bench every day at the same time in hopes of finding her again. I thought back on the first words that we had exchanged. Then suddenly, I thought again of the bookseller, of the book. Had I dreamed that, too? This book, the unfindable perfection, renounced by its maniacal author, who had not only forbidden a reprinting but had tried to recall all remaining copies by asking his friends and relatives to destroy them wherever they found them. I hated him; I called him Rat-face-with-glasses, a manipulator. He'd wanted a detour from reality; he'd wanted to modify the past, to mask his identity. But I'd thwarted his machinations; I would discover his true face and reveal him to the world. Now.

I plunged my hand into my raincoat pocket, and nothing, nothing there.

How many times since, both in dreams and in reality, have I looked for that street, that square, that woman, met at an intersection, as well as the books she spoke of and the landscapes they evoked.

Unattainable things that are all I desire: a book, a woman, a blue flower on a mountain, the fleeting heroine of an unfindable book, all more compelling than their real doubles.

The Chessboard of Dreams

The floor was a Mondrian. Seen horizontally, its orthogonality falls into perfect perspective; the parallels converge at infinity, and the black and white squares become trapezoids. Various randomly placed characters in seventeenth-century dress—heavy shoes and plumed hats—stand around like the sturdy Dutchmen on the flagstones in Saenredam's church, conversing in the wash of light filtered by the small-paned panels of the clerestory. An armed guard sleeps, his back resting against a pillar that makes the corner of a donjon or perhaps a bell tower, while a simpleton in a funny hat turns a hand rattle and mumbles as he walks away down a line as crooked as a drunkard's. Ignoring this flunkey, a chevalier wrestles his rearing horse back into control, and a fat woman armored in a great swoop of hooped skirts heads off in all directions at once, calling out to her husband, who sits on a throne—or maybe it's an easy chair—claiming it all belongs to him and defying anyone to dislodge him.

The guard's whistle, the simpleton's mumbling, punctuated by the jangling bells on his hat, the cluckings and warblings of the indignant fat woman, the raucous laughter of her husband, who, spitting now and then, remains royally indifferent to all the commotion, and the clattering hooves of the recalcitrant horse across the colorful stone floor all add up to a concert of noises, rhythms, and echoes of varying hues and heights that would have merited the name of Klangfarbenmelodie, but would have made one think of Varèse more than of Webern.

Every now and then, Marcel Duchamp's hand moves one of the people. Unaware that they're being moved, they keep up their circus with an arrogance that never questions the mastery of their actions.

Is this a scale-drawing? he asks.

The Duke of Milan,
Leonardo, and the Lying Prior

There are people who incite parables. Their wise words are repeated, their actions made examples, their pedestals erected. History needs stories in order to make itself clear. Leonardo's was one of those lives; not only naturally talented, he was also gifted with enough pluck to make his talents into accomplishments that would instruct the future. And good stories have deep roots; prodigious artists begin as child prodigies.

Who knows whether Vasari invented or reported reality; it doesn't really matter—he serves the cause. He claims that as a child, Leonardo drew constantly and had a certain predilection for the monstrous and the terrifying. Perceiving his talent, a farmer on his father's land commissioned him to paint a scene on wooden shield that he used for hunting. Something really horrible, please, he requested, something that will put the enemy to flight at a single glance or that will, at least, distract a wild boar long enough to let me skewer him. Nothing, swore Leonardo, will out-terrify this shield, and he recalled the story of the Medusa's head, which his father had told him. For the next couple of weeks, he could be seen all over the countryside, armed with net and jar, poking under stones to seize vile beetles, mantises, crickets, and tarantulas, haunting caves (those antechambers of Hell) to tweeze out centipedes, millipedes, and vipers' nests, lurking along the edges of ponds to waylay unwary frogs, salamanders, and catfish, climbing into attics and haylofts to extradite bats, vampire or not, and anything else that lived upside-down. Every day, he'd bring his monstrous loot back to the little shed at the edge of the farm that served as his private studio where he drew and built his strange machines. And there he began by taking the most horrific trait of each of his models—the claws of one, the scales of another, the eyes of a third, a forked tongue here, a fang there—to compose the most frightening thing imaginable. It took him so long that his imprisoned models began dying in their jars, and the stench of their rotting corpses began to inundate the tiny workplace. Passersby held their noses and fled what they were sure was the workshop of a sorcerer, while the boy, buried in his work, didn't even notice.

The following story offers another example: based on hearsay, it was finally written down by Jean-Baptiste Giraldi as an example to conceited poets who think that creativity is based on nothing but the self. Henry Beyle, a lover of edifying tales as well as anything coming from across the Alps, told it again in his history of Italian painting.

The Sforzas were in power in Milan. Had Ludovic, known as the Moor, had his brother the Duke Galeazzo assassinated? Whether he had or not, as his young nephew's guardian, he'd attained the power he'd wanted for so long. When, at the convenient death of that nephew, he became duke in his turn, the Moor's most pressing project was to commission a painting from Leonardo to adorn the large wall of the refectory at Santa Maria delle Grazie, where he planned to put the family tombs. They died a lot in that family.

Tyrants are complex people. If their schemes could be read on their faces, they'd certainly never be given the latitude to execute them; however Le President de Brosses claimed that Ludovic the Moor, renowned for his atrocities, had one of the loveliest faces in the world.

A painter is a physiognomist and a bit psychic. He sees little things that no one else sees until he reveals them. His art is based on his ability to recognize intentions hidden in expressions and to make them serve. In the curve of a chin, the angle of a brow, the gleam of a glance, a portrait reveals all; it's an art that holds reality to account.

Cecilia Gallerani was the most beautiful person in Milan, and the Moor, abandoning his young wife's bed, visited her nightly. And she modeled for the Master; she holds a white ermine against her breast. Not the fur of a dead animal but the animal quite alive. The painter, never short on strategy, knew that by making Gallerani as attractive as possible, Sforza would be flattered. So, considering that sitting is tiresome and that both animal and sitter would be restless, he hired a tambourine player, a flautist, and a clown and told them to stand a bit off to the right and distract the princess by playing airs and making faces. Instead of the dull expression of the bored model, he wanted to capture an expression of attention engaged by a spectacle the viewer would assume is marvelous because it's not shown in the picture. Her face, slightly turned to the side, is lit up; her lips sketch the hint of a smile. The same quick interest also brightens the face of the rodent; his nose twitches and his ears perk up.

No one doubts that images are lies, thought Leonardo, but the truth, whatever else it may be, is also only an image. You have to lie right to speak the truth.

It's said that the ermine was the Duke's emblem, and that as Cecilia had given him a son the very year that he'd married Beatrice d'Este, the painter decided to replace the child that could not be shown in his mother's arms with his father's symbolic animal. The truth is an image.

We don't know whether Ludovic appreciated the allusion, but he certainly never asked Leonardo to paint his own portrait, perhaps for fear of seeing the black lines of his soul leap out under such a perceptive paintbrush.

The Prior of Santa Maria delle Grazie wasn't impressed with Leonardo's work, and he found the man himself distant, arrogant, and not much inclined to gratitude. He would have liked to see the commission conferred upon Montorfano, who'd already done—on schedule and for a good price—the large crucifixion that hung in the refectory facing the Prior's table. However, he was so anxious to please the new sovereign that he vociferously supported his choice, and even managed to give the impression that he had suggested it. But whenever he was alone or with an underling such as Montorfano, he mumbled his resentment under his breath. Yet, on Leonardo's first visit to the refectory, he welcomed him with the warm and protective air he was so expert at adopting, all the while rubbing his hands together like a snake-oil salesman. Leonardo, noticing the permanent scowl he kept hidden beneath his beard, instantly saw him for who he was, and so asked only technical questions. Height, width, composition of the wall, date of the monastery's construction, meal times … Humiliated at being treated like the concierge, the Prior took a deeper and deeper dislike to the artist.

The Monk's Refectory is about ten yards across, and the walls are paneled up to shoulder-height. It was the upper portion of the entire expanse of wall that Leonardo was commissioned to paint, which amounted to a rectangle roughly 30 feet by 15, a double square, susceptible to a pleasing symmetry.

Leonardo was left free to choose his subject. A crucifixion wouldn't work in such an elongated space, not that he wouldn't have enjoyed showing Montorfano what he could do with the subject. A nativity also wouldn't really work in a rectangle of those proportions—not unless one were willing to tack on a phalanx of wise men with an army or two winding back over the horizon. Why not a refectory in the refectory, Leonardo suddenly thought; a scene at a table lined with diners facing the monks, who gathered for their meals along one side of the two long tables that crossed the room—what could be more natural? That decided, he chose the specific moment mentioned in the Scriptures when Christ gathered all his disciples around him on the first day of unleavened bread and announced to the twelve that one of them would betray him and that he would have to leave them. At the same time, he took up the bread and the wine and brought them together to indicate his body and his blood, soon to be spilled. It's a moment full of the sort of suspense and interior drama that makes a good painting, Leonardo thought.

And so he got right down to work. Painting three windows on the wall showing a calm countryside and blue sky, he created a view from the refectory by piercing the back of the picture plane. He placed Christ, lightly sketched, at the center of the great table, directly in front of the middle window in such a way that he already seemed a part of the landscape into which he would disappear just three days later, while he depicted the disciples, evenly divided on his right and left, as solid bodies sitting against the wall. In order to make the painting easier to read, he chose to place the Twelve on the same side of the table, an arrangement most likely not historically accurate, but much more effective aesthetically. Like everyone, he'd read in Mark that the disciples lay back as they shared the Easter lamb, but isn't it better to imply that they were just like us, he asked himself, with a big table and tablecloth, in order to create a more majestic scene than languishing bodies could have done?

The painter rapidly put the protagonists in place, giving each one a particular air or gesture to specify his participation in the event. James the Just stands open-armed as if before a miracle with such an ecstatic face that Christ's, by comparison, seems unmoved. But it's only that Christ has already gone within and is preparing soon to exist only inside everyone. The two disciples standing behind James questioning Jesus look like they can't believe what they're hearing, whereas John, sitting with his hands crossed before him on the table, seems to understand the stated threat and to have left it up to God, while Andrew, in gesture, speech, and expression, is in complete denial. Will it be I? asks young Philip, striking his chest. Thaddeus, Matthew, and Simon, at the other end of the table, are deep in conversation, talking with their hands in a mutely eloquent dance.

Judas he'd only sketched in, sitting in the foreground in front of Peter, leaning on his right elbow while his left hand reached forward to take the bread at the same moment as Jesus. That was the sign that he would betray him. We need signs, though not too explicit, merely suggested.

There came a point when everything was done except Judas' head, which Leonardo hadn't yet painted in. He'd been overheard swearing The bastard, I've got him! Then, The bastard! He's gotten away! And it was said he'd been seen throwing his palette and brushes on the floor and stomping on them. For several days, the painter didn't even enter the refectory; in fact, it seemed like he had abandoned his work. Had he been so revolted by the traitor that he couldn't keep on painting him? The prior saw his objections vindicated. I knew anyone that pretentious would give us nothing but trouble, he said to Montorfano. We'll have to report this to the donor.

My Lord, you have paid that measly painter too much— he's just not up to the job; he's pocketed your money and run off. He's got it all done but Judas, who's nothing but a sketch. The face and head remain unpainted, and all this time, instead of working, your artist is hanging out in disreputable places—people tell me they see him every night, said the Prior.

So the Duke sent his guards out to find the painter. I like your painting of the Eucharist, he told him. The disciples are vibrant, and the Lord is full of compassion. It's all fabulous, but I ordered a finished painting, and I've ended up with a headless, faceless Judas. They tell me you haven't touched the thing for months, that all you've been doing is hanging out in bars and drinking.

My Lord, said Leonardo, they're lying. Since the day you did me the great honor to offer me this commission, not a moment has passed that I haven't worked on my painting. It's the only thing I think about; I dream of completing it, but I just can't quite settle on Judas' face. I'm thinking about it—in fact, I think of nothing else. I've broken my pencil a hundred times giving his nose a good twist, but he always eludes me; it's as if he had the power to keep me from painting him.

Satisfied with this response, the Duke went back to scheming, calming the French threatening his borders, and cavorting with Cecilia. But the Prior of Santa Maria delle

Grazie would not leave him in peace. Every day, under some newly invented pretext, he requested an audience, and after discussing some minor issue, he would happen to mention that they still hadn't seen the artist at his brush.

Ludovic again called for Leonardo, determined to rebuke him.

I have proof, he exclaimed, that you have abandoned your mission. The prior tells me that it's been almost a year since you even came near the painting, and I'm not about to doubt his word.

Lord, if your Prior is a better painter than I, he's welcome to finish the painting, Leonardo replied. Just because he doesn't see me in the refectory doesn't mean I'm not working day and night on the painting.

Don't be absurd, said the Duke. How do you dare claim to be working on a painting you haven't touched for months? The truth is you're enjoying my money, but don't have the integrity to complete the work for which I paid it. They tell me you spend your time drawing gears and hydraulic systems and all sorts of mad contraptions that no one will ever use.

A painter's studio is his head and the world, said Leonardo. You must understand, my Lord, that I don't paint dolls or marionettes, but men dressed in hope, doubt, and distress. Their eyes, their hands speak for them. The faces of Simon and Matthew, both wise men, are done, as is that of young Philip, who's stands behind. His features are borrowed from a page in the palace; they are the embodiment of candor. James the Just is copied off your stable master—did you recognize him? No, of course not, because I made him into another man, and yet it's he. No man is another, and yet every man is all of them, and it's in the gap between that the art of portraiture lies. For Peter's face, for instance, I went back to Vinci to study a farrier, an old friend of my father. Each face emerges from countless studies; I do each one full, three-quarter, and profile. After they've posed, I draw them again from memory. Sometimes a head will strike me because of its shaggy beard or its wild hair or its deformed or extravagant features, and then I'll follow the man for hours just to watch him from every angle. I must possess him. Do you understand that? You who possess castles, armies, ministers, and valets—there's no one you really know. You—you hunt with a falcon, my Lord, and I hunt as well; I have a falcon's eye and a wolf's endless time. Drawing the truth takes not only the hand, but also the heart. My hand must know the slightest curve of cheek or nose, and so well that I could draw it again with my eyes closed. The division of light and shadow across the planes of a face is a subtle art based on rules even more precise than those that govern the war machines that I draw in the margins—and that would assure you victory over the French, if you'd only consent to have them built to my designs.

Ludovic softened; again he was convinced, though he managed not to show it.

I'm not saying I'm not interested in your machines—that we can talk about later—but at the moment, I want a Judas with a head and a refectory with a painting.

For this most complex of faces, that of Judas, the felonious, the avaricious, the traitor that made Scripture come true—what can I say? I simply haven't found the right model. John, here pictured between Judas and Jesus, says that the latter dipped an end of bread into the juice of the lamb and held it out to the former, who ate it. He added, and these are his very words, 'Through the mouth does the Enemy enter.' Satanas. Lord, it is I who must paint the man that, having followed Jesus in utter faith, is suddenly pierced by evil, the cursèd bread. It's a mystery so deep it takes more than a single life to understand. And how can I paint what I don't understand? You've given me solid gold, real silver; I owe you something better than the false currency of appearance. I've got to paint the mystery so that it is utterly clear without losing its absolute mystery. If I've been hanging out in uncouth places, it's because I hope to encounter a man with the features of evil incarnate, but now I see that I've been on the wrong track, and I thank you for opening my eyes. Outlaws have more honor than you'd think, and it's not in some dive that I'll find my man. It's in a place they say is holy, and it's not far from you, my Lord. And since you seem in a hurry to get it done, I don't think it will take me more than an hour to give Judas the stubborn chin and the sly eye of your Prior.

Moonless Night

Brutally awakened by a blazing light that I assumed was day, I was immediately struck by doubt, uneasiness, and then insomnia, so I got up. I looked out the window, trying to find the star that was pouring forth this cold gleam. There was no moon. I went out into the garden. I could see the effects of the light all around me—shadows stretching out from the poplars, a velvety halo around the house—but the light seemed to have no source. I also seemed to hear a bird singing—in an unknown timbre, both sharp and flat, a high note, but muted, veiled. The song didn't surprise me; though I'd never heard it before, I recognized it, and as I went deeper into the undergrowth in search of its source, I noticed that the dead leaves and branches under my feet made no sound as they broke, and it all became clear: it was the song of *the bird that doesn't exist*.

Completely reassured, I went deeper and deeper into the woods and probably fell back to sleep.

Autumn

The Shogun, ever with an eye to increasing his glory, decided to hold a great painting competition at the Palace. Stimulate rivalry, incite confrontation, he thought. In short, pit them all against each other in an effort to please me. News of such a competition, if it's a good one, will spread far beyond our borders, and all the other kings will be jealous.

So announcements were sent to the most distant villages, the most remote monasteries, and even to the huts of hermits. Every painter-poet in the kingdom was required to present himself on the West Terrace on the twenty-sixth day of the fourth moon. The edict demanded that each bring his own materials—a roll of paper or silk, brushes, ink sticks, and inkstones—and register with the lieutenant of the guard upon arrival. When his name was called, each would then improvise a painting on the spot, before the sovereign, the high ministers, and the judges, following it with a poem inspired by the painting, constituting either its commentary or its title. The painters could choose either to create their own poems or to select something from the standing body of literature. In order to ensure true improvisation and thus enable a clear choice of victor, the Shogun decided not to announce the theme of the works until the last minute.

Each painter had his own way of preparing for the contest. One sat on his heels and minutely observed the mountain before his cabin, noting the precise locations of the springs, the uncanny way the clouds veiled the summit just before dawn, and the exact tone of the rocks left open to the sun. He memorized the echoes of waterfalls and the exact shapes of emptiness as it showed itself between trees and the fishermen on the lake, paying particular attention to the relative order of beings and things.

Another exercised for several hours a day in order to keep his wrist supple enough to hold the brush without a trace of stiffness or frailty, thus ensuring that the blacks would not go flat and the colors would ring in all their brilliancy.

A third borrowed a book of models from the Palace library, and on tracing paper made of oiled rice paper, he diligently copied the works of the ancient masters, following their sweeping contours as faithfully as he could.

For his preparation, Hokusai fed his chickens and sat in the shade of a large tree on the banks of the Tatsuta River, daydreaming.

Everyone gathered on the stated day: the women of the court dressed in their finest, the dignitaries adopting the important air they adopt so well, the judges careful not to let their moods show. Preceded by drums and zithers, the sovereign crossed the nine thresholds and took his place, surrounded by his highest ministers. Only then did the Director of Rites reveal the competition's theme: Autumn.

The one who'd prepared himself by closely observing reality thought, Ah, autumn, now that's something I know well because I've seen it. The springs surge up; the mountain is coiffed in white clouds, and crevices and grottoes appear in the rocks because there are fewer leaves on the trees, and the undergrowth is sparser.

He who had exercised his wrist thought, The colors must be utterly transparent to keep them alive; even if autumn has the fragile splendor of decline, the ink must sink deep into the fibers, as does the life force into the slightest blade of grass. The apparent gaps in the composition will echo the leaves missing from the trees and the lacunae in the cloud banks. In order to capture that properly, the brush must no more than graze the surface and never retrace its path.

And the one who had given himself up to copying the ancients tried to remember exactly how various earlier painters had evoked the calm melancholy of the season—just what tone of what color should the moon be? And should the scene be crossed by sparrows or cranes? Certainly, no crickets or dragonflies still hanging around the pond.

Hokusai arrived last, a little late, a basket in his hand and a roll of paper under his arm. He unrolled it across the grass beside the West Terrace and anchored it down with a stone at each corner. He then mixed some blue ink in a little cup, adding a lot of water to keep it fluid and clear, and placed it beside the paper.

Then he poured some red ink, the sort used for official seals, into another bowl at his side, and extracted from his basket, a flapping, squawking chicken, ready for a fight, even though its legs were tied. With a firm grip on the bird, he dipped her feet into the red ink. Then, with a little kick, he overturned the cup of blue ink, spilling it across the paper and into the grass. With a flick of his knife, he cut the ties, freeing the bird, who set off across the paper, leaving behind her a brilliant trail of red.

Hokusai bowed low before the Shogun, saying,

Autumn, the
maple leaves
glide downstream

The sovereign turned to consult his judges and then asked,
What is your name, and what is the name of your chicken?
Clearly, one of you has won, but I have not yet decided
which.

Hokusai (it is said) replied, Sire, in every kingdom in the
world, there are peasants who raise chickens, but only one
sovereign has a humble subject mad for drawing who once
was called Hokusai.

Silhouettes

Silhouette of Herman Melville. Silhouette of Henry David Thoreau. Silhouette of Ralph Waldo Emerson. Silhouette of Nathaniel Hawthorne.

In Concord, in Boston, in Lenox, skating
down the Merrimack River
scarves floating out behind
breath hanging in clouds
as they call out to each other

Silhouette in a window of someone who watches them
from a red house, from the attic,
one hand parting the calico curtains

Silhouette of a whale on the hilly horizon

Silhouette of Robert Walser walking away

Silhouette of Robert Musil walking away

Silhouette of Knut Hamsun walking away

into the snow, gymnastics, exactitude
on Peer Gynt's blue-flowered paths

Silhouette of Ricardo Reiss dreaming that he's no one.

Silhouette of Segalen leaning on the rail of a ship.

Silhouette of Cavafy smoking
an oval cigarette.

Silhouette of the young man he brushed against as he
passed him on a certain day at a certain hour

Silhouette of Velimir Khlebnikov
and his dog

On a beach at the Caspian Sea

Eating caviar gathered from the sand

Silhouette of Sandro Penna.

On the bus.

On a bicycle.

At the port.

Dazzled

by a mocking angel

Silhouette of Witold Gombrowicz

Puffing on his pipe
unconvinced

In Cordoba,
Argentina

nineteen hundred
and fifty-four.

The world is behind him.

Silhouette of Giotto di Bondone
child of Vespignano

engraving the shape
of one of his sheep
with a flint on a slate

Cimabue en route
a bull's head keeping an eye out
sees him from the top
of a hill

and knows him by his grace,
says Vasari

salutes the royalty
secreted inside,
says Foucault

and according to Billi
brought him to the via del Cocomero

Silhouette of John J. Audubon
born Jean-Jacques

leaning over a double
elephant folio
on the banks of the Hudson
listening to the multilingual mockingbird
miming

a creaking door
a tinkling piano
a barking dog

he can't see it in its tuft of yellow jasmine
he says it's the fog on the river
that hasn't yet lifted

Silhouette of Joseph Roth
at the end of his travels
far west of everything
and himself

He smokes another cigarette
in front of a glass of absinthe
the pierced spoon with its poised sugar
in wood by Picasso

a round table
in a Parisian bistro
America
the weight of grace

the Austrian distress
says Morhange, the expert

Silhouette of Friedrich Nietzsche

on the via Po in Turin

he embraces a horse

and the world reels

Silhouette of Jacques Roubaud
on television, hooodbleevit?
lock of hair falling across his eye scarf around his neck
playing Baudelaire in silence
ah youth ah
Jacquelaire Roudelaire Baudelaire
Jacques Roubaudelaire

Silhouette of Ambrose reading

not moving his lips

says Augustine

the spell is broken

the ice age begins

Silhouette of Louis Soutter
crucified, he crucified
with his bare hands
in a black rain
a great black wind in his head
feverishly crucifying
with his fingers
in Morges, in Geneva, in Brussels, in Lausanne
in Paris, in Chicago, in Colorado Springs

Sunken eyes drawn lips sunken cheeks jutting cheekbones
hat on head impeccably placed checked tie held by a pin
hands in his pockets though gloved.

Silhouette of James Joyce, in his fifty-seventh year, with hat and cane, in Paris, in the street, in the rain, in a black and white photograph tinted sepia to look antique, in a book, I remember, in my handwriting, on this page, then printed and slipped, almost bluntly, among others, into your hands.

Silhouette of a peasant seen from the back, Seurat in Comté pencil on Ingres laid paper, she's carrying a basket on her hip and walking away down a road that is not drawn in.

From her bun, a single lock of hair, a strand, escapes.

I recognize the shawl around her shoulders, the basket, the road, the light caught in the furrows of the paper.

Silhouette carrying bread. Silhouette leaning in a doorway. Silhouette walking into a room. Two silhouettes carrying something between them.

Silhouettes that wait. Silhouettes talking not looking at each other. Silhouette sleeping. Silhouette leaving the house.

There are silhouettes that are and there are those that have been.

Pieces

With every intention of eating it, I peeled an apple. Then I cut it into pieces. And then the pieces into pieces, and then each piece into smaller pieces. When my plate was full of very small pieces of apple, I could no longer keep from crying, my heart was too full, it overflowed, my arms fell to my sides, and I sobbed.

John came in and sat down next to me. He said nothing; he let me cry. Then, very softly, he said: It's not you on the plate, or your father, or your mother, or your brother, or your sister Juliette or your cousins René or Marcel, or any of your children. You have cut no one into pieces; as a mother, you haven't been any worse than others; all mothers are wonderful, and as a daughter, you haven't been any worse than others. No one could reproach you on that score, and there's no one you can reproach on that score. These little pieces you've cut up are apple, nothing but an apple cut into little pieces, and you're going to eat it because that's exactly why you peeled it and cut it into pieces, and it doesn't matter whether the pieces are large or small or even very small. Today, they're pieces for a very little girl, but it's a grown girl that's going to eat them. And one after the other, he held spoonfuls of chopped apple out to me as he dried my tears. Then he hugged me, and I hugged him, and I cried again, and he cried too. A few minutes later, I was naked in a hot bath; with one hand, John sponged down my body; he was kneeling, radiant, his Christ's face under all that hair. I was calm; I said: Cleaning up the dead! It was warm, not at all aggressive, grateful. He said: we're going to go to bed and we're going to sleep; it will all be much better tomorrow. He dried me with a large towel and rubbed me down with eau de Cologne. I said: I'm a hundred. He carried me to bed, then he undressed and lay down next to me and took me in his arms and we cried in joy.

Early the next morning, I went down to the studio. John was still sleeping; I could smell his body on me; I was completely surrounded. I started to gather pieces of wood from various sculptures, scraps in various shapes, and I piled, glued, screwed, and wedged them together, making a curious scaffold—very solid with the feel of something about to collapse, full of tiny protrusions, overhangs, misalignments. John came in silently. I said: You see, I put the apple back together again. We laughed.

Then, I wrote to John: 1) *I love you* 2) *bad daughter   bad wife   bad mother* 3) *It's hopeless* 4) *I miss you* 5) *bad woman* 6) *bad life* 7) *where is it all leading?* 8) *I love you* 9) *forgive me*

I tore up the letter. I wrote: Not guilty. Using scotch tape, I put the letter back together. I wrote: 10) *Not guilty   Not guilty   Not guilty.* I put the letter in a drawer and locked the drawer.

Epiphany

The painter was puzzled. He bustled about in silence, washing his brushes in clear, running water, arranging his mortars by size, the smaller within the larger, putting his drawings, studies, and plans in his sketchbook. He kept his hands busy, distracting himself, as he thought over his project.

The canon had requested a large nativity in a single space. Narrative altarpieces were no longer the rage, he'd said, a large fresco, please, across the entire wall of the baptistery; you can come and measure it. Or perhaps an adoration with shepherds and wise men if you want, but for the same price. We're not paying you by the number of horses or camels, but for your power to evoke the divinity incarnate.

We don't want visual tricks, added the canon, an erudite man who spoke in quotations borrowed from the ancients; we want only honest work to help us teach the true faith.

Doctors have written treatises and translated the Scriptures, but their words are often obscure or ambiguous, and we have to interpret them in the pulpit. And most of the people don't know how to read. The paintings that you do, you and your workshop, don't so much decorate our churches as constitute the only books that the illiterate can follow. They are their only guides, and our lessons need these visual aids in order to be fully grasped. Your responsibility is great. As great as the power of images over the imagination.

Divinity incarnate, that's easy to say, thought the painter. Those adept at words have it easy; you imagine whatever you want. They'll always find a way to claim that they haven't said what they've said or excuse it away as "just an image." When those adept at words claim that a phrase is an image, they mean "I said this in order to say that"—a distinction between the letter and the spirit. But I have to chose: to show or not to show. My images can't say anything other than what they are. I have to make the word flesh. What you see is what you see.

Okay, so the project is to paint a baby, a donkey, a cow, and a few shepherds or wise men; I can always manage that. But the thing is the baby. Everyone will know he's God—the manger instantly identifies him as Jesus. Even without manger and wise men, any newborn placed in a church can't be anyone else. Furthermore, the mystery is not that he's

God, no one doubts that; the mystery is that God is a man. That's what I have to show; that's what the canon expects from me. And because the word was made flesh in order to confound those who look for God in appearances only, I have to paint this flesh newly formed with all of its attributes.

Recalling the words of Augustine, the canon had phrased it: Complete in every respect. He insisted upon it: the joy of the incarnation. As the bird sings of its joy in being in the world, our child must swell with joy.

I'm going to paint him smiling, the painter said to himself; that will be something new! Aristotle said that no baby smiles until it's at least forty-one days old, which is to say, not until both the mother and the child are out of danger from childbed fever. Pliny claimed that Zoroaster was the only infant who had ever smiled. If he managed it, thought the painter, it's a trait I must borrow; my Jesus is going to smile on the world. He picked up a sketchbook and drew a chubby face. With a couple of quick strokes, he rounded out the cheekbones, parted the lips, slightly raised the corners of the mouth, and lit up the eyes with dash of white.

Okay, he said to himself, that'll work. But all baby Jesuses painted since the dawn of time have, as far as I know, two arms, two legs, a nose, and two ears. Complete in every respect; the holy man must have meant something else—could he have been hinting that he wanted me to give the infant a tiny penis and two little balls? He was careful not to say so, but he did say complete in every respect, so untangle that one, you who make images.

Christ and sex—the two words seem instantly mutually exclusive. The word sin separates them and keeps them apart. The first is exempt and the second is saturated. And for this very reason, bringing them together in a single image will be the strongest way to create surprise and to strike the senses.

Byzantine icons allowed no sign of the flesh other than a naked foot peeping out under the robe. The Sienese showed the baby Jesus dressed in a long tunic and a philosopher's cloak. Later, he's shown wearing a child's dress that the Tuscan painters at times raised up as far as his knees. Isn't it clear where they were heading? asked the painter. The canon demands more.

Traditionally, German sculptors who carved crucifixes from wood wrapped his loins in linen dipped in plaster. The painter remembered one whom he'd met in his master's studio who'd taken care to give the statue a perfectly proportioned sex before masking it with the cloth. It's not nothing that we're hiding from sight, he'd said. He further reinforced the protuberance by knotting the linen precisely at the desired spot so that the penis might be thought erect in its hiding place. They'd talked about it for hours at the tavern. Claus was a pious man who'd consecrated many years to reading the gospel. He'd worked in Dijon for the Duke of Burgundy and had had the audacity to loosen the Gothic stiffness. The sculpture that made his name was of a group of prophets at the base of a great crucifix—how well he'd known how to fashion the curves and folds with his chisel. The turban he gave Daniel is still talked about, as is the cloth he wound around Jesus' waist. He claimed that the penis he'd carved from pear-wood, the hardest wood he could find, revealed Christ's human nature. He hid it behind the cloth but in such a way that it was still perceptible. He went so far as to claim that his erection should be understood as a symbol of the resurrection of the flesh. In addition, he said, the tension in the direction of the sky gave his composition the extra dramatic force capable of convincing the most skeptical.

The painter imagined that he could do the same with a crucifixion if the canon gave him another commission. A three-quarter view, rather than the usual frontal approach, would allow him to make the knot of cloth stand out from the tortured body against a cloudy background sky. They'd say a strong wind had caught up the linen, mimicking the tension of the flesh toward its resurrection at the very moment of his death. On other days, he violently rejected this idea, finding it exaggerated and overdone, opting instead for a diaphanous cloth that would allow the protuberance to be visible as if it was in the clear waters of the Jordan in the Baptism of Christ painted by his master in his studio in the Via del Cocomero.

But at the moment, it was a nativity that he had to paint for the canon. The painter was ambitious; he dreamt of a large studio and a squad of young assistants. He'd be jealous of their youth, but he'd very conscientiously mentor the most gifted among them, and his name would become known far beyond the province. In order to attract other commissions, he would have to astonish the canon. The painter had the obscure intuition that he would have to dare immodesty. He remembered the Mother and Child that his friend Taddeo had painted in which he drew the Virgin's hand up toward the top of the thighs of the child standing on her knee. The conjunction of the Virgin's gesture and her gaze, probing that of the painting's viewer, could not be clearer: Look at what I'm showing you; understand what I'm telling you; there is the proof of the incarnation, the completion that Augustine demanded is there at the tips of my fingers.

And in this other maternity in which the Virgin watches the child who seizes her breast with two hands to press it into his mouth, while the child himself stares insistently at the viewer, seeming to say: You see, I am human; I suckle; I need earthly sustenance; I am just like you.

To go even further? To disclose all? A naked child, in a stable, at Christmas, it doesn't make sense. Even in Palestine, it's cold on the 25th of December, and loving parents, no matter how poor, would not leave their child naked on a pile of straw. Reason aside, he thought, though it's not natural for him to be naked, at least they'll understand why I've undressed him. In any case, they were destitute, they were fugitives, they took nothing with them. He'd made his decision; he would do what no one before him had done. Pliny said that Polynotos is the first to have painted a woman whose attractions were visible beneath a transparent veil. His paintings have disappeared, but his name remains. A new Pliny is going to write down my name; I will be the first to dare a truly naked child. It would be best if this innovation occupied the center of a large painting, and if everything else was organized geometrically around this small naked body exhibiting its attributes.

Fired up with his new resolution, the painter grabbed his notebook and started sketching out an overhanging rock on which he positioned the Virgin. Joseph would be a little bit further back, leaning on an outcropping. It was more of a cave than a stable, with no donkey and no cow, but from the left and from the right came a great procession, filing down from the top of the painting, winding down the flank of the mountain. Nobles on horseback, their men on foot with their helmets and lances, as if heading out for a crusade. They had come a long way, and some had broken rank in order to hunt deer to feed the crowd. In the foreground, the Kings and their retinues stand closely packed. You sense a shudder, a murmur, reverberating through the assembled. Two or three men in red hats seek out the eyes of the viewer as if to make him part of the action, while others seem to pass the glance on, guiding it into the center of the composition where the eldest King, kneeling, bows deeply before the acknowledged majesty of the child. Next to him on the ground, he has placed his crown and a small coffer. Bare-headed, as a sign of humility, he seems about to kiss the child's foot, which he has taken in his hand. In a gesture that feels quite natural, the mother holds the other leg by the thigh and moves it aside. The child also takes part in the demonstration by lifting the thin veil that falls from his shoulders. But anyone who follows the King's eyes will admit that it's between the child's legs where the small penis, uncircumcised, stands erect that his gaze is rooted. The mother's glance and even the child's are directed toward this clinical confirmation and seem to encourage it. The King knew that a child had been born; the omens had announced it, and therefore he had set out following the star. What he had just verified and then announced to all and that all had repeated was not that a God had been born but that he was a man, and his divine penis standing between his chubby thighs proved it.

The painter closed his sketchbook; all he had to do now was to get down to work. I know that you'll know just what to do, the canon had said. And for a long time after him, it was inconceivable to depict the infant Jesus other than with his attributes fully visible and often highlighted by a gesture or the convergence of the lines of perspective. Until another canon, a hundred other canons, hired a hundred other painters called braghettone to adorn the canvases of masters with veils, leaves, and bunches of fruit in order to mask that which offends stupidity.

And not long ago, in the age of photography, it happened, iconoclasm of prudishness, that before printing the reproductions of famous paintings, they were retouched in order to erase this trace of immodesty.

The Unbeliever

On Sunday morning, Mary Magdalene, anxious to get back to her mourning, rose before dawn and went down to the garden of the sepulcher. She saw the stone moved away, and ran to up Simon Peter calling, They've taken him away, and we have no idea what they've done with him. And then burst into tears.

Who are you looking for, asked a shadow hovering a little behind her. Mary thought it was the gardener, but when the shadow pronounced her name, she recognized him and addressed him as Master. And he: —Don't touch me.

On the road to Emmaus, he slipped in alongside two of his friends as they discussed recent events and joined in their conversation. When evening came, they asked him to come in. It wasn't until he took up the bread and broke it that they opened their eyes and recognized him.

The same evening, he appeared to the disciples, who had locked themselves away, and he spoke to them.

Thomas, known as Didyme, wasn't with them. When the eleven told him their story, he replied, Illusion is the word I give to all desire that isn't palpable, and phantasm to any body created by reverie alone. What passes through doors and walls, I call a ghost; what leaves no imprint as it walks across sand, an hallucination; what speaks without a body, a mirage in midair; and what will not show itself in a mirror, a deceit and a lie.

That which you know, you know, said the luminous body. There's no need to believe it. Add to the world the un-known quantity.

*

Speak carefully of the dead. Again and again. Of their ineffable presence. Bring them to mind. Take care not to bump into them. They arrive, they pull up on our shores. Soundlessly. Soundlessly, to pour the contents of days into the tall, thin bottle of night. To decant substance into form. To clarify. The angels' share. A subtle entropy, a prolonged reach, a sustained tremble, infinitesimal in its repetition and its variation, like Schubert's in the *Streichquintett*. At being's edge or already from the other side, but coming back, slipping in among us, among the interstices that we leave vacant.

An angel passes, its shadow falling across us, signaled by a scent; a silence proves its empire; a resemblance underscores its singularity, superimposing it on the world, transparent, so that nothing of the world is hidden, and nothing halted in the day.

You fear the spirits' judgment, but you needn't. Their remonstrance is pure form. Having lived too much, and being too weak, too evanescent, they appear only when a declivity in the self calls out to them, an appeal. Fillers of the void, they fill the void with void.

I'm an inconsistent Hebrew, says he, believing nothing of it, I believe it.

This is a story; any resemblance to actual people, events, or situations would be as unlikely and as suspect as a resemblance between words and things.

The Words of Others

He no longer knows when it started. He never made a distinct decision. It never passed into conscious thought. By the time he'd become aware of it, it was too late to stop. It had become a part of him. It was as natural as walking or singing or whistling, though accompanied by a vague feeling of guilt, the sense of abetting a hoax. But ah, such a tiny one, who would ever notice? Who even could notice? But is a hoax that goes unnoticed any less of one for that? The sleight-of-hand was real, and perhaps he was its first victim. In short, he no longer knows when it started because it didn't start—it was as simple as that. It had always been this way. The kidnapping, the borrowing, the pillaging had always been, more or less, coincident with writing. Ever since he'd given in to the strange activity of building phantoms and then lending them memories, projects, regrets, and desires, he'd done it by using the words of others. Of course, he'd also used others' lives, taking care to change the names of people and places, to tinker with the anecdotes to make them a little less readily identifiable, but those tricks are, as they say, allowed.

It's like making a portrait, either from memory or from a model, replacing flesh and motion with a stroke that leaves a dash of pencil lead across paper. Does a painter steal his model? Some primitive peoples fear that the photographer steals the soul of the photographed, but isn't it the other way around? Doesn't the portrait, far from taking something away, add to the model? If the portrait is successful, it places the model's soul in a layer over his or her appearance, while in daily life, it's actually quite rare to see people's souls on their faces. Of course, there are exceptions to everything I'm saying, and precisely because they're exceptional, they're no less important than the rule. But normally people don't go walking around with their souls showing: that's the rule for people. Whereas, the rule for a portrait is that if you don't think you see at least a hint of what you could honestly call a soul, the portrait isn't a good one. It doesn't matter whether the painter is great or not—the portrait has failed. And though it may be overly optimistic of me, I'm not even considering the possibility that the model has no soul. Failure happens, even to the best. It even helps us recognize the best. And the best, it's well known, are certainly not free of weakness.

After writing the word weakness, I pause for a moment, look up and gaze out the window, not fixing on anything in particular, but idly listening to the cries of the children playing in the park. Coming back to myself, my eye falls again on the word weakness. Despite the rationalizations that he managed to construct, the analogies with portraiture and other flimsy theories invented for the occasion, he couldn't help feeling a bit guilty for taking recourse in the words of others, the phrases of others, the paragraphs of others—for sometimes it went as far as that—to shore up his inventions, those ordinary situations and characters, more or less similar to the ones that you encounter everyday, but constituted of words. A weakness he put down to a lack of talent, a lack of inspiration (which, they say, doesn't visit the lazy), a lack of application, or simply a lack of patience. And above all, a lack of courage. To an impulse to gain time by stealing materials here and there rather than nurturing them. At the same time, he reassured himself, why not? One might as well shamelessly use whatever is at hand. When Picasso picked up a toy car to make a monkey's muzzle, a cake mold for the chignon of the nurse pushing her baby carriage, or the seat and handlebars of a bicycle to create a bull's head, what else was he doing? One could even claim that material found, selected, and blatantly borrowed is more powerful because it's less labored, more virgin. This didn't keep him from endlessly giving himself grief for lack of imagination and willpower, not to mention ethical feeling. Although he said to himself that a group of words is not, anymore than a single word is, the property of the one who uses it. That all words are by nature the words of others because if they weren't we wouldn't be able to learn them, and even if we could learn them, they would be useless because no one else would understand them. Words are what we have in common, and it must be admitted that it's not with ideas, but with words, that one writes. But these elegant arguments weren't enough to assuage his guilt. He still felt like a thief acting dishonorably, even though only he knew. Insider trading. He felt like he was cheating. He blamed it on his reading, and didn't worry about it too much. And no one else even seemed to notice. Shakespeare, Dostoyevsky, Kafka, Faulkner, Balzac, practically word for word and without even using quotation marks. But quotation marks would have made no sense, for his project didn't have that erudite and slightly pedantic edge of the specialists, who, to give them their due, plaster their arguments with citations deftly chosen from among the authoritative writers in the field. No, his borrowings acted more as points of departure, as trampolines, as engines, as stimulants. By contagion, by osmosis, by mimicry, he could get something started and follow it on out. Or perhaps it was just that an old reflex based in modesty and an aristocratic education that insisted that one never speak of oneself, at least not directly, had here found a way of dissimulating itself. He wrote stories that felt like confessions; the narrator or principal character (depending on whether he was writing in the first or the third person) tended to go around in sackcloth and ashes, accusing himself of errors, impostures, evils, or simply failures. It would have been hard to charge him with painting himself—in the guise of one of his characters, for instance— in a flattering light. Most of his characters were either lunatics or obsessives. But he no doubt secretly feared that these confessions, though ostensibly those of imaginary characters, would be assumed to be his own. Had he thought that systematic borrowing would protect him from egotism? He had taken what he feared others would accept at face value and masked it with a play of forms, and in so doing allowed himself to think that language produces thought rather than vice-versa. As for the rest, hasn't there been cheating as long as there's been language? We're in a theater of shadows, in the realm of false resemblances, where substance is nothing but appearance miming the illusion of a secret truth always stripped bare. And there's always something that continues obstinately to make and unmake these simulacra by weaving, sewing, and splicing together snatches of discourse stolen from here and there. For what is it that makes these stories speak to us and, even more, speak to us of ourselves? They resemble no others and, all in all, give away nothing of the books from which the words that compose them were taken. A utopia streaming along without a pause: in the words of others, you can avoid speaking of yourself, but in such a way that it is entirely your own. Words count less than what they silence, he thinks. In fact, he'd been trying to escape himself as much as to reveal himself. He cultivated reticence. Certainly, it was what he wanted; he'd always wanted to be a writer, yes, but a different one, someone unknown. I am not the one you think I am, was his private password. For him, the world, life, society, even his friends were an insistent request for an agreement he thought it his duty to secretly evade. And he'd found a way to do it—a way as successful as it was inadmissible, and though he reproached himself, he stubbornly stuck to it and made no attempt to stop. In fact, quite the opposite; though he knew it was a dubious process, it had become his true nature, hidden. To betray, deceive, lie—such was now his truth, a truth he might detest, but nonetheless to which he clung like a shipwreck victim does to a chance log that carries him off.

But something's still missing from the picture. Just as a successful criminal, thinking that he's cleverly deceived the whole world all these years, sometimes ends up perfectly arranging the evidence that will allow a deft detective to hunt him down, he decides to own up, to confess his treachery to the all the critics who have praised his work without ever noticing the knavery. He considers the various ways he could do this and settles on suicide, leaving behind a letter detailing exactly what he's been doing—what ridiculous pathos. Or he could unmask himself (since everyone else is clearly incapable of it), by writing an attack on his work under a pseudonym, with all the proof laid out in black and white. A public avowal, on live t.v. and in the evening papers ... but who would he be doing this for? Who cares about such little cases? Go make your books anyway you want, my friend; we'll read them or we won't, and we'll like them or we won't, that's all. Spare us your smelly little secrets.

The Gardener

Dawn comes from the left. The man wears a wide-brimmed hat that shades his face, so you can't see it. The rays of the rising sun form a kind of aura behind the hat. He moves in silence, as if he's barely touching ground. He carries a shovel over his shoulder, or maybe a pick. His complexion is not that of a gardener, nor of a gravedigger—we think of them as small, wiry, knotted men; whereas, he is tall and spare. His smooth hair frames a short beard, and his lips are fine, his glance soft. He has a rather detached air.

Her back to him, a young woman kneels next to a recently opened grave, sobbing. She has put a pot of oil down on the ground beside her. No chignon restrains the disordered hair that veils her face. She mumbles incoherently—something about a stone that's been moved and a corpse no longer there. No one knows where it is, she says, or words to that effect.

The gardener, seeing a woman so distraught, turns to her and says something comforting. Which she hears as the two syllables of her name and recognizes the inimitable way in which her Master pronounces them. She spins around calling out *Rabouni!* and no longer sees the gardener, but in his place, the one whose shrouded body she sought all yesterday in vain. He's as beautiful now as he was when she wanted him. When they were adolescents and played under the trees and in the haylofts. He had refused her with a tender comprehension. Later, she'd followed him in his travels, going along with the others, simply to hear his voice, to stand in his shade.

When she heard her name, she reached out to him. Even if it's a dream, let me dream one last embrace. The gardener stopped and said: Touch me not, but go and tell the others what you have seen.

A cloud slid over the sun. The young gardener put away his tools. On his way back to his father's house, he thought of the woman whose grief he'd found so moving. She'd been so choked with emotion that he hadn't quite caught what she said; perhaps she'd thought he was someone else. As he strode easily along, he watched the sun crossing the hills. He was feeling a little light-headed, a little bit absent. He melted into the countryside.

Marsh

I walked along the path reading *Paludes*. On the other side of the fence, a grey horse walked along with me, matching my steps.

A mental fence.

I got a little bit ahead. He'd stopped to graze on weeds. So he's back again. I hear him munching behind me.

So old friend, not going to make the distance?

He's joined by a brown horse. One barely takes a step without the other.

Oh, but you're working.

Yes, I'm reading.

Oh, you're reading—you're not working.

Whatever you say.

And what are you reading?

I'm reading *Paludes*.

What's that?

It's the story of a shepherd and the passage of time. He invents a field and decides to stay there. He kills birds and roasts them. He goes fishing and doesn't catch anything. Each event reflects a state of mind.

Reading *Paludes* put me to sleep.

Not that it was boring—just a little too much rosé with lunch, no doubt. E. had made steamed sole with julienned vegetables. As we ate, she'd asked me how I'd spent the morning. If I'd worked.

Reading *Paludes,* I told her. To make my reply decisive.

Little daily simulacra.

Ah, the agenda, the agenda.

But, sir, that's precisely what I detest.

All glory to the inventor of forms.

To little marble thieves, to fishermen of pearls.

I'm from the South; I believe in magic, in the transmutation of forms, in the passage of a camel through the eye of a needle.

To stick needles into the body of a little rag doll. To reverse the course of negativity. To revive the ghosts.

I see him again coming up to me, looking sad.

What's new?

Not much.

Where are you going?

Where I was before, but not entirely.

You weren't entirely there before or you're not entirely going there now?

That's it.

He looks up at me, gritting his teeth. Which makes a little muscle jump in his jaw. He's wearing a soft hat, a bit battered. Behind his little round glasses, he looks like André Gide. He looks at you, but not directly. As if he's looking just beyond. There are inner battles, lost causes. You think no one notices, and then a little muscle gives you away.

Are you in pain?

I'm just pretending, but shhh!

In fact, a subtle euphoria runs through you, but you don't want to incite envy, so you force yourself to mask it.

That's it.

Six months later, we buried him.

Will I walk all the way over to the marsh? Will I walk all around it? The problem with marshes is the aggravating tendency of water to stagnate. The surface gets covered with algae. With *conferves,* corrects the author. The sky is no longer reflected—too bad.

A bird snare, a duck blind, to go to ground there, to shelter.

Pieter Cornelis Mondriaan's Sin

The day is coming to a close. The cold, even light of the studio is warmed by a red spot, the setting sun reflected on the opposite wall, the sun that never crosses the open window facing north. A little surge of emotion at the end of the day. A cordial. The flask is returned to the cupboard. A half-glass, no more. The painter is satisfied with his day. He looks at the canvas he's been working on; he has it well in hand; he can see where it's headed. Black lines divide the space, a red rectangle in the upper left, a smaller yellow one lower down on the right. A struggle between figure and ground; they annihilate each other in the victory of the surface, of vibration, of rhythm. He aligns his meticulously washed brushes along the table. Dutch care. And with a twinge of regret, tosses his pencil shavings into the stove.

He's always had a tender spot for these thin flutters of wood edged in graphite or a sliver of color. They improvise a small bouquet in the blue and white china bowl he drops them into, making him think of the traditional Balinese offering of three floating frangipani flowers. Every morning, he watches the fine lacy garlands form as he carefully sharpens all the pencils he used the day before. He tries not to let them break off too early, which means he has to turn the pencil very delicately. And because it's the first thing he does every day, it has, little by little, become charged with superstitions. A pencil sharpened in one smooth move, leaving a beautiful shaving several inches long, is a good omen. The day's work will be bright, alive. He particularly likes the shavings from the yellow pencil; they remind him of lemon zests curling across the folds of tablecloths in the Dutch still-lifes he cherished in the Royal Museum when he was young.

He's often thought of drawing these small wood-petal blooms that open each morning on his table and end each evening flaring brightly and briefly in his stove before disappearing. But he counters this vivid, indulgent wish with the demand that has guided him ever since he chose Vermeer's pure light and Saenredam's austere interiors, which had been relegated to the museum's side galleries, over the still-life painters' exquisite woodcocks and brass cauldrons.

From that point on, he'd looked at nature differently, and when he went out into the fields to paint, it wasn't the eternal cows along the water's edge that he chose, but a tree, a dune, a lighthouse, simple structures that he reduced still further until they began to radiate an unknown light.

His dress and even his physical appearance changed. He shaved his prophet's beard and cut his long hair, combing it back impeccably. He tied his tie, even his bow ties, more soberly, buttoned his coat all the way up, and donned frameless glasses that managed to give him a serious and determined air. Little by little, he renounced even the trees, the dunes, the lighthouses, and, with a tear for Saenredam, the church facades and consecrated himself entirely to the right angle, the black line, and rectangles of primary color. The prestige of the orthogonal, the nobility of pure color: scorning shadow, false depth, and everything that pretends to dimension in order to come to terms with surface without becoming mundane: a painting is not an illusion; it is a fact. Every morning he repeated the articles of his personal catechism, and reaffirmed his commitment to them.

However, every now and then, he let himself relax by painting, usually in watercolor, one or two lilies at the end of their long stems or perhaps the bushy head of a chrysanthemum, sliding the stem into the neck of a bottle in order to hold it up. He'd never had the slightest desire to paint a bouquet of flowers. Stupid, vulgar bouquets. But one flower, one alone, as a figure, a being rising from its ground. Or two flowers, sometimes, as a dialogue, a union, no more. He took an intimate pleasure in rendering, even in charcoal, the creamy white of the lily's curves. This pleasure was not without a tinge of remorse: these flowers, these portraits of flowers, as he liked to think of them, sold so well. Certainly much better than the austere, ambitious compositions he wanted linked to his name for all time. Flower-painting was an old tradition in this mercantile city, where the people, after whitewashing all the churches and renouncing the cult of the Virgin, had instigated the cult of the tulip. Gardeners recruited the best painters and paid them a fortune to create watercolor catalogues of the most beautiful specimens. Their bulbs sold at the price of gold and changed hands perhaps ten times before they flowered.

For a bit of cash to put wood in the stove that burned his pencil shavings each evening, the guilty pleasure of these curves and rotundities; he gave into them parsimoniously, and never tulips—they brought the speculations of the devil too much to mind. Instead, one rose, one chrysanthemum, one lily, from time to time. And he never did draw the pencil shavings in their china cup. All his life, he contented himself with gazing at them affectionately before contritely consigning them to the purifying fire of his stove.

Anthea

The hotel in the Via Partenope was an old one with no charm but its view of the bay. We'd barely put down our baggage before we were off again, heading to Capodimonte for the sole reason of looking one more time at a full-length portrait of an unknown young woman.

The look in her eye.

Spring was just beginning. In the park, the elderberry flowers were already white. From a distance, almost foam. A young couple lay back on the grass; children licked ice cream cones.

On the way back, we got caught in such bad traffic that everything all but froze in place. Cliffs in the city. Promontories. Cornices on arcades. We were practically pinned to the side of the mountain. The look in the eye of the portrait stayed with us. It was both before us and behind us.

Suddenly, traffic cleared, and the taxi dropped us at our door. Night fell.

On a terrace at the base of the Castle of the Egg, we dined on sea bream done in wild water and a bottle of Greco di Tufo. The back label claimed that the soil of Greco, rich in sulfur and calcium carbonate, gives the grapes an aromatic intensity and a mineral fragrance.

—You're reading the label because you have nothing to say ...

—I read labels because an inner demon makes me read anything written that happens to pass beneath my eyes.

—I'm not interested in that demon—lock it up, please, at least when I'm around, though if you've got any other ones hiding out, do let them loose; we might get along quite well.

They call cooking water wild when they've added sparkling Asti wine and a good dose of aromatic herbs— parsley, basil, oregano, fennel, and minced garlic. A dash of oil, and cover. A fish large enough to subdue two people of reasonable appetite should simmer to a perfect pink in about ten minutes. It's a dinner that leaves you relaxed and almost as light as you arrived.

The portrait stayed with us, its black eyes, black hair parted down the middle and encircled by a braid from which hung a broach ending in a pearl. The image still stood, on its canvas, in its frame, behind its glass, on a wall, in a museum, on the top of a hill, but it was also there in the restaurant, with us, behind us, before us, beside us, listening to our idle chatter. Which is the uncanny gift of the fixed image, at least of a few: ubiquity, the paradox of a double nature.

Who was she? What was she to him, the painter from Parma, carried off by his love of the alchemical? We would have liked to know. Of what crime she'd been accused that made her, with her hand poised low on her chest, so silently protest her innocence as she looks you straight in the eye. And how this arm, just slightly completely out of proportion as it starts to come forward, makes her so close, as if the image had been startled out of itself, out of its two dimensions, to take on a body and almost reach us.

Hapax and Apocatastasis

When I was a child, nausea would overtake me whenever I was placed in the back seat of the paternal automobile, and we set off on a long journey, particularly when it was one that led through a pass down into Italy along a winding road. They say it's caused by a conflict between the divergent but simultaneous information sent to the brain by the eye and the inner ear. The first anchors onto the fixed points that constitute the interior elements of the passenger compartment while the second keeps track of the minute sensations caused by displacement in space. Add to this another trouble, the impression of *déjà vu,* a sort of vertigo, not in space but in time, as if a trap opened up in the supposedly stable ground of the present beneath your feet and sucked you in. This detestable feeling comes, not from the repetition of the real but from an immediate and spontaneous perception, faster than consciousness, in such a way that when ordinary conscious perception kicks in a second later, it creates the sensation of a repetition.

While Hieron was the tyrant of Syracuse, Archimedes astounded the prince's court by claiming that, though considerable, all the grains of sand found on all the shores of all the seas are not innumerable. He went on to say that if one can establish the number of grains of sand, it is then easy to imagine a number larger, for example that of all the books that could be written by assembling all the words that can be formed with all the letters of the alphabet submitted to all the permutations conceivable by logic. As this number is finite, it follows that if the human race lasts long enough (and without this optimistic postulate, the whole argument collapses), a moment will come when almost all the propositions that can be stated have been stated, and we'll need to start repeating them in order to continue to give ourselves the illusion of thinking, which will prove Terence's prediction that nothing is ever said that has not already been said.

Gottfried Wilhelm Leibniz, who loved the combinatory art as Uccello did the perspectival, established that if the alphabet had 100 letters rather than 26, the number of all their possible arrangements, both sensible and not, would amount to a 1 followed by 7,300,000,000,000 zeros— a number that's rather long to write out entirely; it would take 20,000 writers 37 years of work if each produced 1,000 pages every year with 10,000 zeros on every page— a tedious job, but in no way impossible in the era, now past, of the accountant-scrivener.

Millenarians, inspired mystics, or lunatic mathematicians, the palingenesis, or universal restitution, has created more than one dreamer. The librarian and aulic councilor of the Duke's court was not the first to be distracted by this illusion as he stood abstractedly watching the river Leine pass under the bridges of Hanover.

Origen and Plato, both natives of Alexandria and one generation apart, developed a common intuition. The first predicted that all creatures would return in the primitive state of purity that preceded their fall into time, and the second professed—or so Porphyrus claimed—that the world is affected by a circular motion that causes the inevitable return of the same things for the same reasons.

Several centuries later, it fell again to a librarian to revive this myth. In the 1930s, Jorge Luis Borges, who wasn't yet completely blind but was already, himself, a living library, chose to ignore his Hanoverian confrere in order to give all the credit to Frederic Nietzsche, who situated the revelation of the eternal return at a precise point on a path in the forest of Silvaplana, at the foot of Mount Julier one afternoon in August 1881. Summer in the Upper-Engadine, with the sun appearing and disappearing intermittently between the rocky peaks and flashing reflected rays off the surface of countless small lakes, tends to engender metaphysical exaltation.

Jorge Luis Borges, who defined himself as baroque (baroque to me, he said, is the final stage of any art during which it displays and squanders its means), is perhaps the first postmodern writer; innovation mattered little to him, as he knew that everything had already been said, but the possibility of revisiting the past with a certain irony remained attractive to him.

Umberto Eco, another walking library, claimed that the postmodern attitude is comparable to the man who, in love with a cultivated woman, wanted to say "I love you desperately" but couldn't because he knew (and she knew that he knew) that this sentence had already been written by Barbara Cartland. The only solution was to say, "As Barbara Cartland said, I love you desperately." By which he meant two things: first, that he loved her and, second, that we are undeniably living in an age of lost innocence.

It takes innocence to seriously believe that we'll one day reach the horizon of knowledge. And it takes no less to chase after hapaxes in a stuttering world. Perspective is blocked; today's Uccellos no longer believe, and we're heading straight for the wall. The sun doesn't reach the bottom of Maloja Pass where Alberto Giacometti balled up the clay with which, an instant before, he had fashioned a head, a head that he had sincerely thought was that of his brother Diego, when all he had to do was to look up at the mountaintops to see it already there, the emaciated head with open mouth and sunken eyes and pointed skull, there for all eternity in rock against sky, silently screaming. Making and destroying are both equally creating, he said, and this winding route that passes and repasses through the same locations of the mind no longer provokes exaltation, but always the same slight nausea.

Persimmons

It was a heavy day. One of inner turmoil. Some days you just wake up like that, for no reason or for reasons too vast, reasons that, when the days are lighter, still exist, but at a distance, their grip loosened.

The evening before had been oppressive, stifling. I'd gone out onto the balcony several times. To breathe. To look at the sky. Weighted with clouds. My sky portended nothing good. The constellations that run our lives seemed to be leading me nowhere. A good for nothing day. Good for nothing but catching a cold.

All morning, I'd wandered around the apartment, unwashed, unshaved, half-dressed, while the cold got settled in. I'd picked up a book, read a few pages, a simple story, the thread of a life. They were playing Honegger on the radio; I sank down into a blob and stayed. It was as if I had a decision to make, as if it was absolutely vital, and yet everything around me conspired to put off the decisive moment, and events were left to take their own irreversible turn.

It was a story about codependence, about traps. A story about staying too long. A story about someone who becomes inescapably entwined with another. It didn't use lofty words, but instead, small, everyday facts, the sort that, every day, add themselves to all that's come before, making links that could have been broken one by one, but taken together form an inescapable chain.

There are shared dependencies, and they can be painful or sweet. In this case, the narrator, a woman, who seemed to be the more dependent, was the one who needed more freedom, more distance from herself, from others, from events.

In fact, she had to get all the way to the end of her story in order to tell it accurately. There was clearly a connection between the stalemate in her writing of the book and the stalemate in the story that the book was telling, which was her story with this man.

This wasn't lost on her. And it was no doubt why she'd gotten herself into the situation and wasn't able to get out of it. In order to thwart herself, to put obstacles between herself and what she took to be her destiny. To play for time, to let it unfold, to see just how far it would go. Shame, ignominy, humiliation; it was awful.

Destiny is a curious feeling, composed of both will and abandon, of restraint and negligence. Neither accidental (it'll happen no matter what) nor inevitable (it could have always been different), destiny feels like the arbitrary caprice of a god. It makes little difference whether you fight it with all your might, try nimbly to outrun it, or simply let its current carry you away.

Except for time. The way you spend time.

Who was it who said that morality is a matter of the way you spend your time.

He beat her. He insulted her, he took her money, and then after she'd given him more, he stole even more. He'd leave her for days without a word and then suddenly come back and start tormenting her all over again.

She thought of him as a son, and she loved him like the son who would have been her lover. She forgave him everything. And all the time, she watched the gangrenous progress inside her, noting every symptom. The book advanced in step with her degradation.

Did she go through it all just to have something to write about or did she write the book in order to justify the horrible mess that her weak character, ineptitude, and lack of imagination had gotten her into—or was it all simply because the stars had decreed it should be so?

That's what disturbed me as I read this otherwise banal story. And that's why I couldn't put it down, and why I read it to the end, all day long, wandering from the bed to a chair, from the chair to the balcony, from the balcony to the kitchen, then back to the chair.

The huge skies, the stretching beaches, and the many, many greys of the Normandy coast, where the story took place, all played a considerable role in the atmosphere that emanated from its lines. A tiny little story enshrined in an enormous setting, a natural setting composed of fine sand, monumental white clouds, and permanent rain. A small grief in cotton and cool water.

One day she slipped her pen into her pocket, gathered up her notes, and left. The man happened to be out at the time, but she thought that even if he'd been there, she'd have done the same. She didn't give a second's thought to his reaction, to what he would do when he came back. She had turned the page.

The first train. To take the first train after so much uncertainty, superstition, and self-abasement is almost comic. That's how the book ends, the train, the landscape out the window, unfurling, changing with an insistent, nagging rhythm, mentally infinite, the wheels on the rails. Suddenly, though they had nothing in common, this book made me think of another one, a deliciously decadent novel in which a man crossing the Atlantic recounts the life of voluptuous pleasure that he has since had to give up. Summer has passed, and autumn, too, what's he got left? A strange taste, the savor of those late fruits that have no flavor at all until they're almost rotten, that we eat only after the first frost.

The radio was still playing, not Honegger, probably Schubert, a piece arranged around a small number of cords. The notes gleaned from the cello were like single drops escaping from a faucet, slowly, the alto sketched a clearing that would then get interrupted, then get taken up again, different, more intense, like a last leap. I left. It was winter here, too, but the sun, as it worked over the vestiges of snow along the sidewalks, seemed sure of itself. Can reading a book or listening to an adagio change even the slightest thing, or is it that, really, we do nothing but wait for the moment when the fruit falls?

I no longer know if I dreamt this or if I read it—I don't think I actually lived it. There are the scenes that have a precision, a presence, a truth that one finds only in books or in dreams. Dreams, books, they're like windows that isolate a bit of reality and offer it up to us, plucked from the ambient chaos, ephemeral marvel, while the dreamer (or the reader) remains parenthetical.

Waves

With the day's work over, we went to sit for a while on the bench in the garden to watch the sunset, which was already staining the farther shore. The languid water, its majestic swell, and the ample expanse of the river all had their calming effect. From where we sat, the sky looked higher, the light finer, and the earth at peace. She followed the passing clouds with her gaze, then the waterbirds playing in the willows' lower branches and the delta of a flight of ducks.

She deciphered nature's signs, calculating their meanings and seeing in them omens both good and bad. She punctuated her predictions with commentaries on the season, claiming it either early or late in relation to some ideal calendar that supposedly made everything come out even.

She also knew how to say nothing. How to let time pass like water through fingers, like a river between banks. A river is made as much of time as of water, she'd say, its banks give it form, but it's a provisional form, a borrowed one. With everything, she said, you have to make a distinction between substance and accident. Form is contingent, while substance, like all that lives, wants only to maintain itself. And that, it turns out, requires imagination.

She's not there anymore, but then neither am I. It's only in thought that I sit on that bench. And who can say but that she, wherever she is today, is also sitting there in thought, thinking about the passage of time, about the cycle of the seasons, and the presence of the dead.

Today, my wrinkles are hers, and those that ruffle the surface of the pond, stretching out toward the shore in concentric circles, are the same as the ones that made me consider the permanence and vanity of all things when I stood there as a child, trying to attract the wary frogs by throwing them a red rag tied to the end of string attached to a peeled branch taken from among the stakes in the garden that Clemence, stooping over, used to tie up the peas that the summer storms routinely battered down.

And their evening croaking—the signal that the sun had passed the horizon, that the chill would soon set in, and that we must leave the bench—is it only in my mind that I still hear them? Frogs, for whom there is no past, nor future, but only, according to a sage who loves paradox, the indubitable instant.

As we sat, she didn't say any of these things. She didn't say anything at all. She didn't discourse on the monads or make fine distinctions between an instant and time's succession or between the permanent and the precarious. And that remains her glory.